Four Stories About the Human Face

Four Stories About the Human Face

Ryan Napier

BULL★CITY
PRESS

DURHAM, NORTH CAROLINA

Four Stories About the Human Face

Copyright ©2018 by Ryan Napier.

Library of Congress Cataloging-in-Publication Data

Napier, Ryan.
Four Stories About the Human Face / by Ryan Napier
p. cm.
ISBN-13: 978-1-4951-7880-1

Published in the United States of America

Cover design and artwork: Sofie DeWulf
Interior design: Molly Weybright with Spock and Associates

Published by
BULL CITY PRESS
1217 Odyssey Drive
Durham, NC 27713

www.BullCityPress.com

Table of Contents

Pink Dolphin   3

A Human Face   21

The Tower   39

The Holy Family   59

Acknowledgements

Burrow Press Review: "A Human Face"

The Cossack Review: "Pink Dolphin"

Noble / Gas Qtrtly: "The Holy Family"

Queen Mob's Tea House: "The Tower"

Thanks to Ross White, Rebecca King Pierce, and everyone else at Bull City Press for trusting in these stories and making them better. The students in Ross's publishing class were sedulous copyeditors. Ben Gwin gave excellent advice on "A Human Face."

I owe to Christine Jacobson a debt that I can barely express and never repay. She is my first and last reader, and if I am occasionally less hapless than my characters, it is because of her.

for Christine

"Hitherto the human face had mixed often in my dreams, but not despotically, nor with any special power of tormenting. But now that which I have called the tyranny of the human face began to unfold itself."

- De Quincey

Pink Dolphin

Something was wrong with my pictures.

I took pictures of the usual things—myself, my dog, my meals. I used interesting filters. Every time a new iPhone came out, I waited in line and bought it.

And still my pictures were bad.

I posted my pictures on Instagram. Other people liked them and wrote nice comments. But I could tell: something was wrong. My pictures were not like other people's pictures.

I scrolled through Instagram and saw my pictures above and below other people's pictures. My pictures stuck out. Other people's pictures were alive. Their selfies and dogs and meals hummed with reality. I could see that these people had full and complex lives, which their Instagrams only hinted at. Their pictures were the tips of icebergs—little pieces of something big and deep.

I wanted to be big and deep too. Every time I took a picture of my face, I hoped to see a strange creature— something I didn't recognize, some new species. The picture always showed a white man with a big nose.

All my pictures were like that. My dog was just a fat old

pug. My meals were just vegetables and pieces of meat. My life was just my life.

But why? I was a normal guy. I had a job and an apartment and a college degree and a girlfriend and debt. I was like other people. But my pictures didn't look like other people's pictures.

I couldn't understand it, and for a long time, I was unhappy. I took my phone to bed with me and scrolled through Instagram for hours, looking at other people's pictures. I hated looking at other people's pictures, and I loved looking at other people's pictures. The scroll was infinite. I fell asleep holding the phone. Sometimes, as I drifted off, it slipped from my hands and hit me in the face. I was tired in the morning, and my face was bruised and sore.

I wanted to change. So I took more pictures—pictures of my tattoos, the sunset, old pairs of jeans, interesting graffiti, other people's tattoos, fireworks, the beach, old factories, trees, the flag, brick walls, full moons, old barns, clouds, my legs, my girlfriend, my knees, my kitchen.

When I took a picture, I looked at it immediately, searching it for depth and reality. Depth and reality were never there. So I took another picture.

If I could—somehow—take just one good picture, the infinite scroll would stop.

Somehow. That was the problem. I didn't know how to be deep. I scrolled and scrolled.

And then there was Haitun.

• • •

My girlfriend was a consultant. People consulted with her. She traveled all over the country, consulting. And now her company was sending her to an international conference of consultants in Haitun.

I read about Haitun on my phone. It was a big city in southern China, on that strip of coast where the Europeans had built their colonies. The English had Hong Kong, the Portuguese had Macau, and the Dutch had Haitun. At the end of the twentieth century, the Dutch had given Haitun back to China, and now it was one of those cities of the future—miles and miles of towers and money.

I looked at pictures of Haitun on Instagram. There were windmills and pagodas, skyscrapers and sea, baskets of dumplings and bowls of noodles. It was all so strange—like nothing I had ever taken pictures of before. I scrolled and scrolled, and then I came to the pink dolphin.

It was on National Geographic's Instagram. The picture showed the tail of a dolphin, sticking out of green water. The tail was pink like candy. The pink dolphin, said the caption, was found only in Haitun Bay, at the mouth of the Pearl River. It was one of the rarest creatures on the planet.

I looked for pictures of the pink dolphin on Instagram. There were a few others, most of them out-of-focus—pink dots in the distance. I tried to keep scrolling, but that was it: there was nothing else to scroll. The pink dolphin was one of the rarest creatures on the planet.

When my girlfriend came home, I made my announcement. I was going with her to Haitun.

She mentioned my debt and asked if I had enough money for a trip across the world.

"I have credit cards," I said. I was disappointed in her. Money didn't matter. This wasn't just a trip. This was my life, my happiness, my reality.

I couldn't stay mad at her. I was too excited. To celebrate, I ordered Chinese food. A man on a bike brought us little white crates of rice and chicken. I arranged the crates on our table and took a picture. It was as bad as my other pictures. The crates were just paper, the dinner just rice and chicken. But I was happy. It was one of my last bad pictures. Soon I would get away from here—and away from myself. I would take new pictures and have a new life. The windmills and the pagodas, the skyscrapers and the sea, the pink dolphin—these would be the tips of my iceberg.

● ● ●

We landed in Haitun at night. I took a picture of the skyline over the wing of the plane, and then I looked at the picture. The skyline was just metal and glass and light. My first bad picture in Asia.

Our hotel was a tall glass building. It looked out onto two other tall glass buildings. As soon as we got to our room, my girlfriend fell asleep. I lay there in the dark and scrolled and scrolled. It was morning in America, and my friends were posting their first pictures of the day. I saw so many good pictures, and I was very happy. Soon, I would be like them. I was so happy that I kept scrolling. I wanted to see more and more of my future.

● ● ●

The next morning, I woke up late. My girlfriend had left for her conference.

I was here now. I was ready to see. How would I find my pink dolphin?

I read the internet on my phone. I found a company that gave dolphin-watching cruises. "ONE OF A KIND TOURS," said the website. They took you to the mouth of the river in a little boat, and you waited for dolphins. "NO GUARANTEES," said the page. "ONE IN FIFTY TOURS SEE A PINK DOLPHIN. PINK DOLPHINS ARE EXTREMELY RARE."

I was very excited.

I called the company. A woman answered. She spoke English in a funny way—too many D's and L's and Z's. Was she Dutch? Was this how Dutch people talked? I listened to her, and I got even more excited.

"No tours today," she said in her funny way. "The water's too choppy. Try again tomorrow."

"I will," I said. But I wasn't so sure. Maybe I would find my real picture today. Maybe I wouldn't even need a pink dolphin.

As I dressed, I read TripAdvisor on my phone. I found all the best things in the city, and I marked each one with a pin on Google Maps. And then I went into Haitun and took pictures.

I went to the harbor and took pictures of the old Chinese ships and their big red sails. I went to Oudestad and took pictures of the stone windmill. I went to the Temple of the Eight Thousand Buddhas and took pictures of the statues and the pagodas. I went to the market district and took pictures of the neon Chinese signs.

As the sun went down, people set up plastic tables in the street and piled them with stuff—spices, DVDs, old cameras, ceramics, little red books, underwear. TripAdvisor told me that this was the night market. I walked through the crowds and took pictures.

The wooden boats were just logs. The windmill was just rocks. The Buddhas were just paint and plaster. The neon was just lights in tubes. The night market was just junk on tables. I was just a tourist.

● ● ●

I left the night market and walked south. I was meeting my girlfriend for dinner.

I came to a long, crowded street. Red paper lanterns were strung overhead. It smelled like gas and vegetable oil. My phone said that this was Tseun Tsan, the famous street of outdoor restaurants. There were hundreds of them—storefronts, each with a stove and a few plastic tables.

My girlfriend was easy to find: she was blonde, and we were in Haitun. She was sitting in a plastic chair at a plastic table.

The owner showed us a picture menu. We pointed to things, and he cooked them for us. We ate dumplings from a wooden basket and eel and noodles. I took pictures. The dumplings were just blobs of dough. The eel and noodles were just long pieces of slime. I posted the pictures on Instagram and frowned.

"What's wrong?" asked my girlfriend.

"Nothing," I said. I had never told her about my picture problem. I couldn't explain it to another person. I barely understood it myself.

She looked at me. Her eyes were very large. I loved her, of course. We had been dating for a long time—since the iPhone 3, at least.

I picked up my phone. I had an idea—an inspiration. "I want a picture of you," I said. "Here."

I had taken pictures of her before—bad pictures. But now we were in Haitun. We had brought our love across the world. Our love would be my iceberg.

"Wait," she said. She did things to her hair. I watched her, and I was sure it would be a good picture. Her hair fell on her shoulders, and the red lamps glowed behind her. She was so beautiful, and she was my girlfriend, and we were here, and I loved her.

I took the picture and looked at it. It showed a woman with yellow hair and a small nose and lots of teeth.

●●●

I woke up late again. My girlfriend had already left for the conference.

Tourism and love had failed me, but I still had my pink dolphin. I called the tour company. The funny woman answered, and spoke again in her funny way. I wondered again if she was Dutch. Maybe she was Chinese. Was this how Chinese people talked?

She told me that there were no tours today. "Try again tomorrow.

I looked outside. There wasn't a cloud in the sky.

"The sun doesn't matter," she said. "If it's too choppy, we don't sail."

I tried to explain. I had come from across the world. So much depended on the pink dolphin.

"You want to see animals?" she said. "Go to the Malao Country Park today. See the monkeys. And then come see the dolphin tomorrow."

The monkeys? The Malao Country Park? I hadn't seen that on TripAdvisor. Did it really exist? I asked the woman where it was. She gave me the number of a bus and told me to ride it to the end of the line.

So I did. I sat on the bus for a long time. I looked at my phone and followed our progress on the map. We were headed north, toward the border with mainland China, toward the high green hills.

I searched the internet for information about the park. It didn't even have a Yelp page. Was there something wrong with it? Was I even allowed to go there? I was scared and excited all at once.

I found one website about the park—the official Haitun Tourism Board page. In bad English, it told me that the Malao Country Park had the oldest trees in the city. It also had monkeys. In the nineteenth century, said the website, there was a great craze for monkeys. The Dutch imported them from Borneo as pets. But when the monkeys grew up, they became too big to handle, their owners released them into the Malao forest. The monkeys had thrived. They had outlasted the Dutch.

The bus left me at the bottom of a steep, curving path. I started to walk. The skyscrapers behind me were tiny, and the trees ahead were massive.

At the top of the path was a big wooden sign. "BEWARE!" it said. "MONKEYS!" There were smaller signs below it in Dutch and Chinese and English: "Monkeys can be aggressive. Do not make eye contact." I took a picture of the sign—another bad picture, just paint on wood.

The path branched in several directions. I picked one and walked. The forest smelled terrible: the monkeys had left little brown messes all over the path. I walked very carefully.

The forest got darker and darker. The trees seemed to fuse together over my head. Soon I couldn't see the sun. I turned my phone to flashlight and held it in front of me as I walked.

And there he was. He was sitting in the middle of the path, in a spot of sunlight. He had a red face and an angry red thing between his legs.

I didn't make eye contact. I pointed my phone at the monkey and looked at him through the camera.

I took a picture. It showed a little furry thing surrounded by brown piles. Slowly, I moved closer. The monkey looked at me. He was very still.

I was looking at him too. I took a step forward, and another, and heard a little squish. I looked down, saw the brown stuff on my shoes, and jumped back.

I dropped the phone.

It landed between me and the monkey. For a moment, neither of us moved. I reached for it first, but the monkey was faster.

He held the phone with both hands, and the glow lit his face. I stood on my tiptoes, trying to see the screen. The fall had hit the "flip camera" button. The monkey was staring at his own face on the screen. He looked at it for a long time, and I watched.

He opened his mouth and showed his teeth. So did the monkey on the screen. He got scared and pawed at the screen, and the phone clicked. The monkey dropped it, screeched, and ran off the path, into the darkness.

I picked up the phone and wiped his fingerprints off the screen. The phone had clicked: the monkey had taken a picture. I looked at it. Most of the picture showed the palm of his hand. But there, in the space between his fingers, were his eyes. There was so much in those eyes—confusion and fear and curiosity and anger. I looked at those eyes, and I glimpsed his whole monkey life—his poor Bornean ancestors, pulled from their homes; his days of climbing and hunting in the deep dark forest; his animal joys and struggles; his long life interrupted by an American with a strange flat device.

Even the monkey was an iceberg.

●●●

When I got back to the hotel, I called the funny woman again. "How does the water look for tomorrow?"

"A little choppy," she said. "But we'll sail." She told me to come early: the tour was very popular.

I arrived at sunrise. The company's office was near the harbor. Their boat bounced nearby in the waves. The office wouldn't open for another hour. The door was behind a metal shutter covered in Chinese graffiti. I didn't take a picture. There was only one picture I wanted to take now.

A line formed behind me—white people with backpacks, Asians with umbrellas. The line spoke English and German and Chinese and French. A few of the people had selfie sticks: they took pictures with the rising sun at their backs. Most of us scrolled through our phones. A young German couple behind me looked at their own pictures. I peeked over their shoulders. The pictures were good.

At eight, a woman came and raised the metal shutter. "Come in," she said.

I knew her voice: she was my funny woman. I looked at her face. Was she Dutch or Chinese? I couldn't tell. She might have been both, or neither. She was unrecognizable, somehow. I could imagine all sorts of different lives she might have had. I was sure she took very good pictures.

We followed her into the office. She sat at a desk and asked how many tickets I wanted.

I looked behind me. The office was very full. We would all be together—all on the same boat, all taking pictures of the same dolphin. All of these people and their good pictures—and me.

I asked the woman if she offered private tours. She shook her head. The boat, she said, stayed out all day. Sometimes it took seven or eight hours to find a pink dolphin. The company only gave one tour a day—that was why the tickets were so expensive.

"I'm willing to pay," I said.

She squinted.

"It's me," I said. "The guy who kept calling. I went to the park," I said. "I saw the monkeys. It didn't work. I need to see the dolphin. By myself."

She kept squinting.

"I'm serious," I said. I took out my wallet and fanned my credit cards in front of her. I was serious. Money was no issue. This was my life, my happiness.

She shrugged. "You could buy all of today's tickets," she said. "It would be *very* expensive." She took out a big calculator, pushed some buttons, and showed me the number. She was right: it was *very* expensive.

She reminded me that there were no guarantees. One in fifty tours saw a pink dolphin. But what choice did I have? I had come all the way around the world, and I wasn't going to return without a good picture.

I handed her all my cards. She swiped them, one after another, and they were declined, one after another. I had a lot of debt. Finally, we found a card that worked. The woman gave me all of that day's tickets—each with a drawing of a pink dolphin leaping out of the waves.

The woman stood and announced to the rest of the line what I had done, first in German, then in Chinese, then in English. I stood there, holding my stack of tickets. The rest of the line said things to me, first in German, then in Chinese, then in English.

The other people were not happy. I wished I could make them understand. They were unhappy, yes—but they were not as unhappy as me. They could go about their days in Haitun, taking good pictures and living deep lives. I could not. They were other people, and I was not.

Not yet.

The engines started, and the boat crawled across the harbor.

There were rows of benches on the deck—empty except for me. The crew did boat things. The funny woman was the tour guide. She stood at the front of the boat and spoke into a microphone. She said that it would take us an hour to reach the mouth of the river, where the dolphins fed.

She started to tell me facts about the harbor. I asked her to stop. Facts only helped me to recognize things. I had come around the world to get away from facts. She turned off the microphone.

One of the crew came to me with a snack cart. I bought a Diet Coke and scrolled through Instagram.

It was hard to look at my phone. It kept moving up and down. I tried to drink my soda, but it was moving too. Some of it went in my mouth, but most went on my face and my shirt. The whole boat was moving—bouncing on the water.

"Can we do less bouncing?" I asked the woman. She shook her head. "Let me guess," I said. "Choppy water."

I tried not to think about it. I scrolled and scrolled. When I took a drink of my soda, I held my phone out at arm's length, to protect it from the spilling soda. I had already had one close call in the jungle. I wasn't going to come all this way and then damage my only way of taking pictures.

We left the harbor, and the bouncing got worse. The little bit of soda that had made it into my stomach started to rise. I felt it, waiting, at the back of my throat. I stared at my phone.

The woman told me I looked green. "Stand up," she said. "Watch the horizon."

It was too late for that. The soda was definitely coming back. I shook my head very quickly.

"Over the side," said the woman.

I pushed my phone into her hands: I didn't want to drop

it over the side. It was like handing over my arm or my ear. *Be careful!* I wanted to shout. *My life is in your hands!*

I didn't shout that, of course. I couldn't. I was leaning over the side of the boat, and the soda was falling into the sea.

It fell for a while, and then it stopped. I looked up and saw a long brown river narrowing toward the horizon. We had come to the mouth of the river, to the place of the pink dolphins.

●●●

The boat stopped. We bounced in the waves and waited.

We bounced a lot. I was sick once or twice an hour. My stomach ran out of soda to throw into the sea, but still I was sick.

The woman still held my phone. "You have to give it to me as soon as we see the dolphin," I said.

She told me not to worry. The crew had a high-quality digital camera. They took pictures of every dolphin they saw. "Don't worry about taking pictures," she said. "Just look. When we get back to the shore, you can buy one of our high-quality digital prints."

"Oh no," I said. "No, no, no." I asked her to put the digital camera away—to keep the crew from taking pictures. "It has to be me," I said. "Only me."

"The prints are high-quality," she said. "Much better than an iPhone picture."

She didn't understand. I didn't blame her. I was the flattest man in the world. No, not even the flattest man—the flattest *primate*. How could anyone else understand that?

But I didn't need her to understand. I needed her to act. So I kept talking, asking, pleading. Finally, she took the camera from the crewman and put it into a trunk in the middle of the deck.

● ● ●

The sun moved over our heads and then fell to our left. Still, we bounced and bounced and waited.

"Can you throw them some food?" I asked the woman. "Some bait? What do dolphins eat?"

The boat didn't have any fish. But the snack cart had some premade tuna sandwiches wrapped in plastic. I bought them all. One by one, I unwrapped the sandwiches and dropped them into the sea, and one by one, the sandwiches broke apart and sank. The smell of tuna filled my nose, and I was sick again.

The sun was now halfway into the ocean. The light deepened, and the brown river changed to purple and red. The woman touched my shoulder and told me that the boat had to go back.

"The sun's still up," I said.

"I'm sorry," she said.

"Ten more minutes."

"Only one in fifty tours see a dolphin," she said. "They're very rare. You could try again tomorrow."

I refused. I had bought all the seats. I had bought all the sandwiches. I had bounced for hours and hours. I had given everything in my stomach to the sea. No—I had earned a dolphin.

She spoke to the crew in Chinese. "Ten more minutes," she said. "That's all."

We stood next to each other at the railing. We looked out at the sunset.

"What is it like?" I said. "The pink dolphin, I mean."

"It's pink. You've seen the pictures."

Of course. If she could have told me, I wouldn't have needed to come to Haitun at all. It—the real thing, the secret of depth—was unspeakable.

We watched the sun for a while. I counted the seconds, hoping that my counting would slow them down. And then someone shouted in Chinese. The woman went very stiff. "They saw it," she said.

"My phone," I said. "My phone."

She gave it to me, and we ran to the other side of the boat. The crew was at the railings, pointing. I raised my phone, framed the dolphin, and pushed the button.

The screen glowed. I looked at the picture.

There it was. It was there. A dot of whitish-pink in the purple-red water.

The tickets and the sandwiches, the sickness and the worry, the debt and the pain—these were supposed to be my iceberg, and the dolphin their tip. But they weren't. Nothing was anything.

I took a picture, and then I took another. I pushed the button again and again. But the dolphin remained a dot in the water.

I knew that there must be another way. "It's just sitting there," I said to the woman. "What if it jumps? Can we make it jump?" I regretted using all the tuna sandwiches.

It was there, and I was here. I wished I had a selfie stick. If I could just get close enough, I could make a long perfect chain—dolphin, phone, self. But I didn't have a selfie stick. So I improvised.

I put my right foot on the railing, and then my left. The crew shouted. Two of them grabbed my legs. "Yes," I said. "Good. Steady me." I stretched out my arms as far as I could. It hurt. I tried to keep stretching. It was almost close enough now. I held the phone by my fingertips. Slowly, I moved one finger toward the button.

The boat bounced. I fell forward, and the crew pulled at my legs. The phone jumped from my fingertips, and my pictures fell into the sea.

●●●

It was ten o'clock when I got back to the hotel. I opened the door to our room and saw my girlfriend, still in her conference clothes, holding her phone to her ear. She looked very tired.

She dropped the phone onto the bed. "Oh, thank God. I called and called."

My poor phone—ringing alone at the bottom of the sea.

She hugged me. I winced. I had spent ten hours on the boat, and I was very sunburnt. She went to kiss me, but stopped. "Your nose." She touched the bandage lightly, and I hissed in pain.

"I think it's broken," I said. My voice was flat and wheezy. "The boat bounced. I fell. I almost went over. The crew kept me on board. But my face hit the railing. The woman bandaged me."

"Broken? What woman? What boat?"

I didn't want to explain. My stomach was empty, my skin burnt, my nose smashed, my face bruised, and my phone at the bottom of the sea.

I fell onto the bed and made an awful noise. Everything hurt, but my nose hurt most of all.

My body was still bouncing to the rhythm of the boat. The bed seemed to rock, the ceiling to scroll by infinitely.

My girlfriend sat on the bed. "I think you should go to the hospital," she said. "You look terrible."

You look terrible—the words opened up some wonderful hole in me. They were a hint of something. My heart sped up.

I smelled something strong and metallic. Blood—and hope.

"Let me see your phone," I said.

"I can look up the hospital—"

"No, no, no," I said. I held out my hands. She gave me the phone.

I opened the camera, held the phone in front of me, and took the picture.

I looked at it for a long time. I tried to understand it.

The white man with the big nose was gone. He had been replaced by burnt pink skin, purple lumps and bruises, wet red bandages.

I stared at that face. I could not recognize it. It was not me. It hummed with some strange reality.

The skin was not just skin. The bruises were not just bruises. The blood was not just blood. Beneath them were huge depths.

But depths of what? Pain, disappointment, pride, anger—those were big words, but none of them were big enough. I did not know what was in the depths. That was how I knew they were really deep.

I was very happy. It had happened, somehow. I was other people.

The bed continued to rock. I closed my eyes. Everything hurt, and I was very grateful. I no longer missed my phone. I knew it was happy—as happy as I was. It was ringing at the bottom of the sea, among the rocks and the dolphins.

A Human Face

I got my dream job—social media assistant at DiPaulo's, the world's second-largest producer of authentic Italian pasta sauces.

It was a big responsibility. I wrote posts on Facebook and Tumblr and posted pictures of the sauce on Instagram. But most of all, there was Twitter. For Twitter, I created Pauley.

I started with a jar of DiPaulo's Old World Style Marinara. I glued a pair of googly eyes above the label. Then I went to the crafts store and bought bright-orange construction paper and a packet of pipe cleaners. I cut the paper into happy, rounded shapes—two big ovals for the ears, one big crescent for the smile—and pasted them onto the jar. The final touch was the pipe cleaners. I found a thick black one, cut it in half, and stuck one half above each googly eye— two eyebrows, raised in wonder.

The face looked so happy. I took a picture. Pauley was born.

Pauley was the profile picture for the DiPaulo's account. On Christmas, I put Pauley in a Santa hat. On April Fool's Day, I gave him a pair of glasses and a fake nose. On September 11, I drew a little tear in his eye.

All my tweets were written as Pauley. If a woman posted

a picture of herself in the kitchen, Pauley replied, "Wish I was there!" If someone talked about bread or pasta, Pauley retweeted it and wrote, "That would taste great covered in me!"

Pauley posted recipes and gave advice. If someone was sad, he sympathized; if someone was happy, he celebrated. He talked about real struggles. He wrote, "When your friends make pasta sauce without you," followed by eight crying emojis. He asked questions. "What's your favorite way of cooking with me?" People shared their answers, and he liked every reply.

Everyone loved Pauley. He had thousands and thousands of followers. He was the subject of two BuzzFeed lists. In a negative world, Pauley was something positive.

In the bad old days—before social media—advertisements weren't interested in people. All they wanted to do was sell you something. But things were different now. I cared. I connected. I related. I gave pasta sauce a human face.

●●●

One day, my boss called me into his office. He congratulated me. Pauley now had two hundred thousand followers. I was very happy.

My boss said that he had a reward for me. DiPaulo's was sending me on a trip.

The company had recently expanded to Eastern Europe. Our sauce was now sold from Paris to Moscow. "The Eastern Bloc is eating it up," said my boss, "with one exception—Narodistan."

I opened Google Maps and found Narodistan. It was a little oval at the edge of the map, a pearl in Russia's ear.

"The economy was weak in the nineties," said my boss. "But they've had ten years of growth. They should be ready for us, but the sauce isn't selling."

He showed me the Narodi branch's Twitter page. I couldn't read a word—everything was in Narodi—but I could tell it was bad. They posted once a week. No pictures, no retweets—not even a single emoji.

They needed my help.

• • •

I landed in Narodistan at sunrise. The capital was in a valley, and the sun rose over the mountains. I took pictures through the window of the plane. All my followers agreed: it was very beautiful.

Seryozha met me at the airport. He was my Narodi counterpart—the man who managed DiPaulo's Narodi Twitter. His beard had big patches of gray around his jaw, and his eyes were always halfway closed. He wore jeans and a t-shirt and a blazer.

We shook hands. I had made my first Narodi friend. I asked Seryozha for a picture. I leaned in close and held up my phone. I smiled; Seryozha squinted.

"I'll send it to you," I said.

Seryozha drove us into the city. Traffic was heavy, but I didn't mind. I was seeing a new country. I took amazing pictures.

We got to the center of the city, and traffic was even worse. We went fifteen minutes without moving an inch. Seryozha rolled down the window and smoked a cigarette. From far off, I heard the sound of human voices, someone chanting through a megaphone. "What is it?" I asked. "A concert?"

"A protest," said Seryozha. He started to talk about Narodi politics—something about the opposition and the elections. It was all very complicated. I started to feel uncomfortable.

Politics are just like the old advertisements—nasty and negative. Politics are another way of selling you something. If we only listened to each other—if we could only connect—then we wouldn't need politics at all.

●●●

We made it to Seryozha's office. A secretary brought us tea and flaky pastries stuffed with onion and mushrooms, and we got to work.

I opened DiPaulo's Narodi Twitter page, and Seryozha translated some of the tweets.

"DIPAULO'S PASTA SAUCE IS THE MOST DELICIOUS PASTA SAUCE," said one.

"DIPAULO'S PASTA SAUCE HAS THE MOST FLAVOR," said another.

The most recent tweet was "BUY DIPAULO'S PASTA SAUCE AT THE SUPERMARKET."

I was disappointed. Seryozha shrugged. "I told people to buy the product," he said. He bit into a pastry. Flakes of it stuck in his beard. "It's advertising."

I explained how social media was so much more than advertising. Advertising is about authority. But no one wants an authority figure yelling at him, telling him what to do. People don't want bosses: they want friends. And we can be their friends.

Seryozha took a big bite. Flakes of pastry fell onto his jacket. One of them drifted through the air, across the table—straight toward my phone. I flapped my hands, and the flake floated away.

"There are lots of ways to connect with people," I said. "One of the best kinds of tweet is the question. For example, you say, 'What is your favorite way to cook with DiPaulo's?' Or

'What is your best memory of DiPaulo's?' You ask a question, people answer, and you start to build relationships. Let's give it a try. Give me a question you could ask your followers."

Seryozha scratched his beard. "Maybe, 'How much pasta sauce will you buy?'"

"Well, okay," I said. "Not bad. Tell you what—I'll give you one of my own questions. A classic. When I asked it, I got over three thousand responses. Ready, Seryozha? You can tweet this one yourself. Here it is: 'Hey America, which do you love more: red or white?'"

Seryozha stared.

"What's wrong?" I said. "Is it hard to translate? Of course, you can replace 'America' with 'Narodistan.'"

"This tweet is not a good idea, I think."

"Trust me," I said. "People love to have these little debates. It's how we engage with them. Besides, it shows brand diversity. Marinara versus alfredo—the classic dilemma."

Still, Seryozha argued. He raised all kinds of objections. He still had a lot to learn. I told him that I was the expert. I told him to trust me. "Look," I said. "I'm supposed to train you. But I also have to report back to corporate. If the report is bad, they're going to fire you. I didn't want to tell you that, but there you go. I say this as a friend, Seryozha."

"Hey Narodistan," Seryozha wrote, "what do you love more—red or white?"

● ● ●

I had flown all night, sat in traffic all day, and argued with Seryozha all afternoon. I was tired. Seryozha drove me to my hotel.

We hit traffic again. Protestors filled the streets, chanting in rhythm.

My hotel was in Skrypsyz Square. The famous Hotel Viy. "The finest hotel in Narodistan," said Seryozha. "Very European."

On the walls of my room were framed pictures of the Eiffel Tower, the Leaning Tower of Pisa, and Big Ben.

From my balcony, I looked down onto the orange bricks and the round gold churches of the square. It was very beautiful. I took a picture.

The protestors were also in Skrypsyz Square. The crowd stood in a little circle at the center of the square, around a statue of a tank.

I lay on the bed and closed my eyes. I was tired, but I couldn't sleep. The protestors had megaphones. Their shouts shook my windows and walls, my pictures and furniture. The Eiffel Tower, the Leaning Tower of Pisa, and Big Ben vibrated to the rhythm of their chants.

I opened Twitter, made a few posts as Pauley, and checked the Narodi account. There was our question. In two hours, it had gotten almost a thousand likes. I loved Narodistan.

I scrolled through the replies. Seryozha had taught me that red was "chrveniy" and white was "beliy." Almost every Narodi voted for "chrveniy." Some of them even posted pictures, proudly holding a can of DiPaulo's Old World Style Marinara.

That was strange. Americans had split down the middle—half white, half red. The results didn't matter, though. Voting mattered. We were engaging people. We were connecting.

I closed my eyes and slept very well.

● ● ●

I woke a few hours later. Someone was knocking. I looked through the peephole and saw the bottom of Seryozha's beard.

I opened the door. There were three men—Seryozha, a very large man, and a man in a blue suit with no tie. The very large man grabbed my arms. He ran his hands up and down my legs, patted my pockets and chest, nodded, and went into the room. He searched the bed, the closet, the drawers, the suitcases.

"Hey," I said. "You shouldn't be doing that."

He kept searching.

When he finished, he nodded again, and the other two entered the room. Seryozha sat on the bed. The third man— the man in the suit—smiled. His teeth were very white, and his hair was very short and neat. He looked young—my age. His cologne smelled like lemons and leather.

He spoke to me. "I'm sorry," I said. "I don't speak Narodi."

"It isn't Narodi," said Seryozha. "It's Russian."

"I don't speak Russian either."

"Really?" said the man. "I was sure you did. I was *certain* you did." (His English was very good.)

"I told you," said Seryozha. "He isn't FSB."

"No?" said the man. He looked at me. "You're not FSB?"

"I don't even know what that is."

"Then what are you?" said the man. "CIA?"

"Is this a joke, Seryozha?" I said. "Is this a Narodi prank— to accuse your American friends of being in the CIA?"

Seryozha squinted at me. I stared into his droopy eyes, and I saw that he had never pulled a prank in his life.

"If you aren't CIA," said the man in the suit, "then what are you? Who do you work for?"

"DiPaulo's."

I unlocked my phone and showed him the DiPaulo's Twitter page. I explained Pauley. I started to show him some of my most classic tweets, but the man in the suit was impatient. He said something to the large man, who crossed the room in two big steps and grabbed me by the shoulders. I squirmed, but it didn't matter. The man was very large. He sat me on the bed, next to Seryozha.

Our faces were reflected in the glass of the Big Ben picture. My eyes were huge with fear, my forehead damp with sweat. Seryozha squinted.

"Do something," I whispered.

Seryozha opened his mouth. I waited. He let out a huge yawn. A flake of pastry fell from his beard, fluttered in the air, and landed on the back of my hand. I did not dare move.

The man in the suit spoke louder now. He asked why I was in Narodistan. I showed him what Seryozha and I had posted on Twitter. Our question now had six thousand responses. I nudged Seryozha in the belly. "I hope you'll trust me next time," I said.

"Incredible," said the man in the suit. He turned around, saw his own reflection in the Big Ben picture, and smiled. "You really understand nothing. Incredible." He shook my hand with both of his. "You're doing wonderful work. Keep it up. I may need you again soon. I'll be in touch."

He turned to go. "Wait," I said. "Who are you?"

"I'm on Twitter," he said. "Your friend can show you." The large man opened the door, and they were gone.

Seryozha was still sitting on the bed. I asked him to explain.

"They came to my house and asked about the tweet. I told them about you, and they wanted to meet you."

"Yes, but who are they?"

He pointed at the window.

I went to the window and looked down into the square. The crowd had grown.

Someone shouted outside the hotel. I saw the man in the suit leave the lobby and walk into the square. The crowd opened for him and his clean blue suit, and he walked all the way to the center of the square, to the statue of the tank. Someone tried to hand him a megaphone, but he pushed it away. He didn't need it. Even on the twenty-ninth floor, I could hear him.

• • •

Seryozha explained it all. I tried very hard to listen, but there were so many Narodi names and so much Narodi politics. It all made me uncomfortable.

In the nineties, Narodistan had a revolution. They kicked out the Russians and won their independence. The leader of this revolution was an army officer named Skrypsyz. He was very popular in Narodistan. After the revolution, he became the president, and he was still the president today. He formed a party called Our Narodistan, and they held almost all the seats in parliament.

The symbol of the party was a white rose.

Narodistan did have an opposition party. Its leader was the man in the suit—the man who had visited my hotel. His name was Aleksiy Litso. Seryozha showed me his Twitter. He had pictures of the protests, videos, retweets. He was very good at Twitter. "You could learn a thing or two from him," I said to Seryozha.

In the last few years, Aleksiy's party had grown in popularity, and the opposition was expected to make big gains in last month's election. But at the last minute, Skrypsyz had cancelled the election. The protestors in the square were calling for a new election.

Their symbol, of course, was the red rose.

"When you say 'white or red' in Narodistan," said Seryozha, "it means something. You asked people to vote, so of course they think you support the Reds."

"I wish you had told me that before we sent the tweet," I said.

"I tried," he said. "I told you all about the political situation."

"This isn't about politics, Seryozha! This is *important*!"

I went to the window and looked down into the crowd. Some of the protestors were holding cans of DiPaulo's Old World Style Marinara. "This is bad," I said. "We don't want to be involved in politics. That's not what we stand for."

"So then we delete it."

"Of course not," I said. "The first rule of business: nothing is ever a mistake. Everything is a chance for us to do something great. After all, the Chinese use the same word for 'crisis' and 'opportunity.'"

"In Narodi, we have two different words."

"Well, yes, in English too. But you're missing the point. We did what we wanted to do. We connected with people. Now we have to figure out how to turn that connection from politics into something productive."

I didn't know how to do that. I needed to sleep. I told Seryozha we would meet again in the morning and plan our strategy.

"Listen," he said. "If I go home, I will have other visitors. They will not be so nice as Aleksiy was. They will not want to talk."

I told him to stay. We were friends. He smoked a cigarette in the bathroom, and we shared the bed. We closed our eyes, but neither of us could sleep. The crowd was still growing, and Aleksiy's voice was very loud.

"Are you a Red or a White?" I said.

Seryozha coughed. "I miss communism," he said. "There were no advertisements."

We woke to the sound of chanting. The crowd had grown.

Seryozha drove us to his office. We walked through the doors, and the secretary let out a little yell. She spoke very quickly in Narodi. Seryozha's eyes opened almost all the way.

The secretary led us Seryozha's desk. The drawers had been removed, their contents dumped on the floor. All the pens had been snapped, and the big blue stain on the carpet was still wet. Even the desk calendar had suffered: someone had torn off all the days, one by one, all the way to November.

Seryozha's computer was missing, and in its place was a note—a few words written in Narodi. "It says, 'Fix it,'" said Seryozha.

We checked Twitter on our phones. The post had thousands and thousands of likes and retweets. The American media had found it. "DiPaulo's posts incendiary tweet in Narodistan," said one headline. "This pasta sauce company is starting a revolution in Eastern Europe," said another. I was too scared to check my email.

"We have to delete it," said Seryozha.

"Now we *can't* delete it," I said. "Now it would be even more embarrassing. No, let's stick to the plan. Trust me, Seryozha. I created Pauley."

We needed to engage more people. We needed to reach the Whites too. If we connected with them, we could connect everyone, and then all the politics would stop.

I wrote a tweet, and Seryozha translated: "Thanks, Narodistan! We saw all the marinara lovers—now show us how much you love DiPaulo's Extra Cheesy Alfredo!"

We watched the replies come in.

"Thank you America for supporting our struggle!"

"Red over white! Down with Skrypsyz!"

One man posted a video. He stood in Skrypsyz Square and held up a jar of DiPaulo's Extra Cheesy Alfredo. "This is how much I love white!" he said, and he smashed the jar against the bricks.

Soon everyone was posting videos. The streets of Narodistan ran white.

"Why are we only getting protestors?" I said. "Why aren't the president's supporters replying?"

"The president's supporters are old people," said Seryozha. "And working people. Farmers, miners, you know. People outside the capital. They don't use Twitter."

I was shocked. My boss had said Narodistan was a developed country.

● ● ●

We kept watching the replies. Aleksiy posted his own video. He had his jar of white sauce, and he smashed it against the statue of the tank. He jumped back just in time to keep his suit from being splattered with alfredo.

He added a hashtag—#MarinaraRevolution.

We had to respond. It was bad optics, to have people breaking our jars. "We need them to stop," I said. "But we also have to stay positive. Tell them to be kind. But also to be amazing."

"It isn't working," said Seryozha.

Twitter wouldn't load for me either. We ran around the office, asking people to open Twitter. It wouldn't load.

"Must be down for maintenance," I said. "It'll be back in a few minutes."

"Facebook too," said Seryozha. "And Google. They're blocked."

"Blocked? Can they do that?"

"Of course. It happens sometimes. During elections, protests, that sort of thing."

For the first time in my life, I felt political. "Seryozha," I said, "your government really is evil!"

I had to leave. I tried to change my flight, but even the travel websites were blocked. I called the airline. A customer service representative would be with me in fifteen minutes.

I faced the wall. I thought of Pauley. What would happen to all the connections I'd made? People were tweeting pictures of bread and pasta, and I wasn't responding. Everyone would be so disappointed. And next week was Thanksgiving. If I was stuck here, without the internet, who would put Pauley in his pilgrim hat? I wanted to cry.

Someone took the phone out of my hand. I turned. We were surrounded by men in blue uniforms and gray caps. Two of them held Seryozha by the arms.

They spoke to us in Narodi. Seryozha did not translate. The meaning was clear.

• • •

The men brought us back to my hotel room. They pushed me and Seryozha inside, and shut the door behind us. I looked through the peephole: they were there, standing guard.

"How long can they keep us here?" I asked.

"Forever, I hope," said Seryozha. "Maybe the internet will never come back on."

My heart jumped into my throat. "Do you really think so?"

"Of course not. It always comes back. But we should enjoy our freedom while we can." He took off his shoes and lay on the bed.

A few hours later, the men opened the door. They gave us

room service—chicken cutlets, baked potatoes, chocolate ice cream. I was sick to my stomach, so Seryozha ate both meals.

I opened my laptop for the hundredth time. I tried all the sites again—Twitter, YouTube, Google, Facebook. Nothing. I could load Narodi government websites and ESPN.

I tried Yelp. My heart soared: they had forgotten to block it! I created a page for Narodistan and gave it a one-star review. "If you are reading this, I am trapped in Narodistan," I wrote. "Please alert DiPaulo's Authentic Italian Pasta Sauces, or the U.S. Embassy."

Days passed. The room service kept coming.

I spent hours on the balcony, looking down into the square. The orange bricks were stained with DiPaulo's Extra Cheesy Alfredo. The sun cooked the sauce, and the smell of old alfredo drifted up to the room.

Still, the crowds were growing. They chanted and chanted, day and night. The walls and the furniture and the pictures vibrated. On the third night, Big Ben fell off the wall and shattered.

The next morning, a fleet of buses drove into the crowd. The buses were full of police. The doors opened and the officers attacked the crowd, but the protestors fought back. They chased the police away. Most of the officers ran into our hotel. The protestors cheered and sang. They turned over the buses and lit them on fire.

Seryozha was sleeping on the bed. "Don't you want to see this?" I said.

"I *have* seen it," he said. "Aleksiy is not our first opposition leader, you know."

"What happened to the other ones? Did Skrypsyz—" I couldn't even say the terrible words.

"He made them," said Seryozha, "members of the government." He rubbed his fingers together. "He made them very rich."

Seryozha was cynical. But I was positive. I had faith in Aleksiy. He was good at Twitter. He knew how to connect with people.

●●●

On the fourth day, the men told us to dress nicely. We were going to the presidential palace.

I gave Seryozha one of my dress shirts. It was very tight on him. He inhaled, and I worked the buttons into their holes.

The palace was at the top of a big hill. Long ago, it had been a cathedral. Its thin stone spires went up into the clouds. I asked the men to give me my phone. I wanted to take a picture.

The men led us to a large room with long red curtains. The stained glass window was shaped like a rose. At the center of the room was a wooden table, set for two. One chair was empty. In the other was a tall man. He was looking down at his phone, his face glowing.

We approached the table, and the man looked up. I recognized him—Aleksiy! He was wearing a tie now—red and white stripes. It looked good. He shook our hands, and I smiled and smiled. "But shouldn't you be at the protests?" I said.

"The protests are over," said Aleksiy. "We won. I've been here, talking to President Skrypsyz, and we've reached an agreement. He's appointed me vice president."

"And the elections?" said Seryozha.

"One has to make concessions, of course," said Aleksiy. "Compromise is key."

"But what about the internet?"

"It will be back on soon. But we had an idea. The protests

have hurt some feelings. But President Skrypsyz and I want to get past that. We need to start connecting with people again. And that's where we need you two."

He told us the idea. He was a genius, of course.

A few minutes later, the door opened. All the policemen saluted. Aleksiy gave a little bow. It was President Skrypsyz himself.

The president sat at the table, and Aleksiy joined him. A cook entered with a steaming pot of spaghetti. He spooned it first onto the president's plate, then onto Aleksiy's. Another cook followed. He held two cans of DiPaulo's—one red, one white. He poured the white sauce onto Aleksiy's plate, and the red onto Skrypsyz's. The cook turned to go, but I stopped him. "Leave the jars," I said. I placed them on the table, and turned the labels to face the camera.

Aleksiy and the president picked up their forks, and Seryozha took the picture.

I thought hard. I had to write a good caption. This was it—the real thing, the triumph of connection.

Seryozha tweeted the picture, along with my caption: "Red or white? With DiPaulo's, you don't have to choose!"

● ● ●

Skrypsyz Square was quiet. Most of the protestors had gone. A little knot remained around the statue. "Why are they still here?" I asked.

"They still want an election, perhaps," said Seryozha.

I felt sorry for them. Elections were all well and good. But an amazing moment had just happened. These poor protestors were too concerned with petty politics to enjoy the connection that was happening. There are all kinds of joy and goodness in this world, but some people refuse to see it.

Seryozha and I stood together in the hotel lobby. We watched the police push the last few protestors out of the square. Everything was peaceful. For the first time, I could really see the beauty of the city. I took a few pictures. My followers all agreed: they were beautiful.

Seryozha shook my hand. We took one last picture together. I told him I would return to Narodistan someday. I wanted to see the country properly. "Next time," I said, "we'll have no protests, no political problems to worry about."

"I would not bet on that," he said.

Poor Seryozha. He was cynical. But the cynical are the most naïve people of all.

●●●

My flight left at dawn. The plane sat on the runway, and the sun rose over the mountains. I tried to take a picture, but there was too much light. The picture was white, empty.

The pilot told us to turn off our phones. I checked Twitter one last time. I had a private message from Aleksiy: three smiley faces—☺☺☺—and a link.

I clicked it. The page opened. In that moment, I knew: I was right and Seryozha was wrong. The bad old days were gone. Things had changed in Narodistan.

The link took me a Twitter page. A new account, opened just a few minutes ago—@skrypsyz. The profile picture showed the president's smiling face, his eyebrows raised in wonder.

I clicked the button in the corner. I was his first follower.

The Tower

I loved her, and she loved me. We were in love. We were a very happy couple—everyone said so.

We were married in the last week of May. We rented a horse farm west of the city, at the foot of the mountains. The snow had melted, and the mountains glowed green.

Our family and friends and coworkers sat on white folding chairs in a field. We stood in front of them, beneath a wooden arch, and promised to love each other, husband and wife, for the rest of our lives. A photographer crouched by my knee, his camera clicking away.

After the ceremony, we went into a big tent. Our family and friends and coworkers formed a line, and one by one, they congratulated us. We thanked them for coming, and they told us how beautiful everything was.

"It's the happiest day of your lives," said my aunt.

The photographer stood behind us, clicking.

• • •

My wife and I spent the night at the farmhouse. The house

was green and white, with narrow windows and a high gable. From our bedroom, we could hear the sounds from the pasture—the hooves pounding the grass, the horses galloping in the dark.

We were very tired. I turned out the light, and we checked our phones one last time.

Her mother—my *mother-in-law*, now—had posted wedding pictures on Facebook. There we were—crying, smiling, dancing. The pictures had a lot of likes and comments. Everyone said we looked really happy.

"It's the happiest day of our lives," I said.

"What?" said my wife.

"The happiest day of our lives. That's what my aunt said."

"Oh," said my wife. "I think I remember that." She looked at her phone. "The rehearsal, the ceremony, the reception—it all runs together."

I put my phone closer to my face. There was a picture of me eating cake off my wife's plate. I guess I had eaten cake off her plate at some point. I looked really happy, eating that cake. I must have been happy.

"Did you feel happy?" I said.

"What do you mean? Look at the pictures. We both look so happy."

"Right. But at the time? Did you feel it then?"

"Yeah. Of course. I think so. It's hard to say."

"It all happened so fast," I said.

She scrolled through a few pictures. "I guess that's why you get the photographer. You're too busy to feel it all, as it happens. But then you see the pictures, and you realize how happy you were."

We looked at our phones.

"It can't *really* be the happiest day of our lives," I said. "That's depressing, when you think about it."

"Of course not. We'll be happier than this."

"We're going on our honeymoon."

"We'll slow down."

"We'll enjoy it."

"Of course we'll be happy. We're going to Charivaria."

We looked at our phones for a few more minutes, and we fell asleep very quickly.

●●●

We had discovered Charivaria on the internet.

It was in an article called "Ten Unforgettable Honeymoon Destinations You Have to See!" The article was a slideshow— ten pictures of ten different unforgettable honeymoon destinations.

The picture of Charivaria showed a high cliff jutting out over the sea. At the edge of the cliff was a tall, narrow tower made of white stone. The tower seemed to hang there, at the edge of the cliff, to float over the water.

It was perfect and beautiful—like something out of a Disney movie. It was a place where a princess might stand and look at the sea and sing, or where a knight would climb to meet his love.

We had looked at a lot of these slideshows and seen a lot of unforgettable honeymoon destinations, but none of them seemed as unforgettable as Charivaria.

We googled it and found that Charivaria was an island in the Mediterranean. It had a very complicated history. I read the Wikipedia article twice, and I still couldn't figure out who was in charge of the island today. (It was either France or Italy or Britain or the Prince of Charivaria—or some combination of them.) At one point, Charivaria had been a Roman colony, and in the Middle Ages, it was ruled by a group of

Crusaders—the Knights of St. Martin. It was the Crusaders who had built the tower. The legend said that from the top of the tower, you could see all the way from Spain to Jerusalem.

We scrolled through Google Images. We saw Charivaria— its beaches and forests, its towers and cathedrals, its caves and ruins, its French cooking and Italian hospitality.

How could we *not* be happy?

● ● ●

The morning after the wedding, her father drove us to the airport. I sat in the backseat, and they talked to each other.

This is my wife, I thought. *This is my father-in-law.*

I kept thinking that. *This is my wife. This is my father-in-law.* Those words had meaning for me now. It was very interesting.

We flew to Paris and changed planes, and soon we were high over the Mediterranean. From our window, we saw the sea beneath us, blue in all directions. For a long time, there was nothing but blue. Then a dot appeared on the horizon. We put our faces to the window and squinted, hoping to see the tower.

● ● ●

Our room was on the thirty-ninth floor of the Charivaria Hilton. We dropped our bags on the ground and stared at the bed.

We had been on two long flights, and we had not slept at all. The bed was very large and piled with pillows. We stood there, staring.

"We can't," said my wife.

"No," I said. "It's two in the afternoon. If we sleep now, the jetlag will only get worse."

"And it's our honeymoon. We didn't fly across the world to sleep."

We agreed: we were going to go out into the city and enjoy ourselves. My wife wanted to change her clothes. I went onto the balcony.

Our balcony faced the sea and looked down onto the old fort. Flags flew over the walls of the fort—the British flag, the French flag, the Italian flag, and, biggest of all, the flag of Charivaria, yellow and white stripes crossed by the sword of St. Martin.

I stood there, leaning on the railing, watching the flags blow in the wind. I closed my eyes, just for a second. The sunshine warmed my face, and I felt myself drifting—somewhere, toward something.

I jolted awake. I shook my head a few times, pulled myself off the railing, and went back into the room.

My wife was sitting on the bed, purse in her lap, asleep. I stood there. After a few seconds, she twitched and opened her eyes.

"I wasn't asleep," she said.

"I know. I wasn't asleep on the balcony."

I splashed water on my face, she did some stretches, and then we went down into the city. We were in Charivaria, and we were going to be happy.

•••

We weren't going to the tower—not yet. We had decided to save it for our last day in Charivaria—it would be the climax of our trip.

Instead, we went to the cathedral.

We walked along the wall of the fort, picking the flowers

that grew between its stones, until we came to a big square. The cathedral loomed over it, casting its huge shadow on the pavement below.

The square was full of outdoor cafes, their tables shaded by green Peroni umbrellas. We sat at a table, ordered two espressos, and looked up at the church.

"I read about this on Wikipedia," I said. "It's significant, for some reason. The architecture, maybe."

"It's Gothic," said my wife. "I think. I used to know this—Gothic, Romanesque, Baroque. I used to be able to tell them apart."

"It has a spire. I think that means it's Gothic."

"Is it a spire? Or a steeple?"

"Oh. I don't know. Maybe?"

"Is there a difference?"

We sipped our espressos. The spire (or steeple?) cast a long shadow, a thick black line that divided the square in half.

I took out my phone, typed "What is a spire?" into Google, and tried to read the results. But looking down at the phone was hard. Gravity pulled my eyelids further and further down.

When I woke, my face felt funny. I looked across the table: my wife was sleeping, espresso in hand. I tapped her elbow, and she woke up. She looked at me and laughed. I had fallen asleep on the table, and the metal grid had left its pattern on my face.

"The coffee didn't work," she said.

"We just need to stay on our feet."

We left a few euros on the table and crossed the square, walking in the shadow of the spire (or steeple?). Above the door of the church was a stone arch, carved with the heads of hundreds of little angels and devils. The angels smiled, and the devils grinned. We passed beneath them and into the church.

It was a massive building, full of light. Two rows of high

white columns ran the length of the church, from the door to the altar. We squinted upward, trying to see the tops of the columns, but they disappeared into a blur of white stone and sunlight.

We walked a few laps around the church. The walls were lined with tombs—stone boxes with sculptures of the dead lying on top. Most of them were knights—the old Crusaders—dressed in their armor, clutching long stone swords. My wife and I leaned over the tombs and read the names aloud to each other.

There were other tourists in the cathedral. They took pictures of the tombs, the columns, the stained glass.

"Do you want to take some pictures?" I said.

"Not really."

"Me either."

We bent over another tomb.

"But we probably should," she said.

"Yeah," I said. "Probably."

"It's the first day of our honeymoon."

"I know. I'll regret it, if we don't have the pictures."

"And our parents—they'll want to see."

"We'll only take a few."

"The bare minimum."

"We'll take more tomorrow. When we're enjoying it more."

We stood in front of columns and statues and windows, and we took pictures of ourselves. We even stopped a priest, gave him our phones, and asked him to take our picture. (He didn't speak English, but we acted it out, and he got the point.) He tried to show us the picture, but my wife and I didn't want to see.

"I'm exhausted," said my wife. "I bet I look terrible."

"I probably still have the table-grid on my face."

We sat in one of the pews.

"Just five minutes," said my wife.

"We're just resting our legs. That's it."

I leaned my head back and tried to see the ceiling through the sunlight. I squinted and squinted, and soon my eyes were closed.

We only slept for an hour. It wasn't even a deep sleep. I had a dream about horses, but it was very short.

When we woke, we felt even worse. Our bodies were as heavy as stone knights. Our legs had fallen asleep. We helped each other to stand and dragged ourselves out of the cathedral.

●●●

We watched the sunset from our balcony. The sun fell slowly into the sea, and the water turned wine-purple. It was beautiful—and even more beautiful because we knew that when it was over, we could go to bed.

The sun set, the sea went black, and we went inside. I turned out the light, and we checked our phones one last time.

"Did you post the cathedral pictures to Facebook?" said my wife.

"No," I said. "Did I?"

I had.

"I don't remember doing this it all. I was half-asleep. Force-of-habit, I guess. How terrible do we look?"

We scrolled through the pictures. They had lots of likes and comments. Everyone said we looked so happy, that we must be having a great time.

And this was the strange part: we *did* look so happy. We were smiling and holding each other, the stained glass glowing behind us, the columns rising up infinitely. The drowsiness, the discomfort, the table-grid on my face—those were all gone, replaced by this strange happy couple.

"I wish I was there," said my wife.

It didn't make any sense, but I knew exactly what she meant. I wanted to be there too. I wanted to feel what that strange couple was feeling.

"I wasn't unhappy," she said.

"Me either."

"It was just another blur."

"Maybe it's like jetlag," I said. "When you fly across the ocean, your body has to catch up. And maybe when something important happens to you—like marriage, like Charivaria—your insides have to catch up."

"It's only our first day."

"Exactly. There's always—" I yawned. "There's always tomorrow."

●●●

The next day, we went to the beach.

The sand was white and soft, the water calm and blue. We rented chairs, lay in them, and listened to music on our phones. My wife looked very beautiful, and I told her so. She said I looked pretty good myself. We had both spent a lot of time at the gym, to prepare for the wedding.

The jetlag was gone. The sun and the wind played across my chest and my legs. I was here, on a beach, in unforgettable Charivaria, with my beautiful wife, at the beginning of our life together. I was very happy.

Wasn't I?

That night, we ate dinner at the hotel. We traded phones and looked at the pictures we had taken at the beach.

There I was, sitting in my chair, listening to my music. There I was, standing in the sea. There I was, strong and smiling.

I looked so happy.

And I was. I *had* been happy. But had I been this happy? There was something excessive about these pictures. They showed some little chunk of my own happiness that I couldn't remember, a bit of it that I didn't fully feel at the time but that had nonetheless been captured by the camera.

I wanted to be there. I didn't want to go back: I didn't want to be there *again*. I wanted to be *really* there, fully there. I wanted to feel the happiness that the picture showed, the happiness that people saw when they liked and commented.

I turned off the screen and put the phone on the table. My wife had already done the same.

● ● ●

On the third day, we went to the Roman ruins. We walked between the broken columns and under the old aqueduct. On the fourth day, we took a bus out of the city and into the hills—the wine country of Charivaria. We wandered through terraces of grapes, and we drank wine poured from the cask. The fifth day was for the market. We went stall to stall, haggling with the merchants, buying jewelry and assorted leather goods.

We took pictures.

I had a good time. I knew I was happy. But all the same, I couldn't help thinking about our pictures. I kept wondering if I was happy enough, if I was getting it all, if the pictures would again show me the little chunk I had missed.

Each night, we turned off the light and checked our phones one last time. Each night, we saw the likes and the comments, and the impossibly happy faces of that strange couple. Each night, we wished we were there, in the place we had been.

We looked at them, that man and that woman, that husband and that wife. We zoomed in on the pictures, and we put our faces close to our phones.

What did they have that we didn't?

"Are we being dumb?" I said.

"Yeah," said my wife. "But that doesn't change anything."

It was dumb. But we still felt it.

We tried to change our pictures. We made stupid faces—stuck out our tongues, twisted our shoulders, scrunched our heads into our necks.

It didn't work. We got even more likes and comments. Our friends and family and coworkers told us we looked playful and happy. And they were right. Even in the bad pictures, there was something that exceeded what we had felt at the time—that stubborn little chunk. We saw those pictures, and we wanted to be there, making those stupid faces. We wanted to be ourselves.

"There's always tomorrow," I said.

"There's only two more tomorrows."

That was true. But I wasn't worried. We still had our tower, waiting for us.

●●●

On the sixth day, we went on a day cruise. There was a small island, half a day from Charivaria, with some interesting rock formations and a waterfall.

The sun had just risen, and we were in our room, dressing.

"I had an idea," I said. "It might sound a little crazy."

"Is it about the phones?"

She had thought of it too. I knew I loved her.

"No phones today," I said. "No pictures. We'll go out into nature. We'll have a natural day."

"It could be interesting."

"I feel bad, of course. It's our honeymoon."

"We want pictures. We want to remember it."

"But all the same, we want to *feel* it too. We want to be present—fully present."

"Remembering doesn't matter if you didn't make a memory in the first place."

We turned our phones off, put them in the room's safe, and walked to the dock.

●●●

It was all too much.

The enormous sea. Charivaria behind us, sinking into the horizon. The schools of silver fish that jumped around the boat. The other island, with its interesting rock formations—fingers of stone grabbing at the sky. The waterfall, splashing onto the rocks. The sun, passing through the falling water, bursting into rainbows. The thousand other details that flooded our brains.

We sat at the base of the waterfall, letting the water hit our bare feet. We watched the other tourists take their pictures.

"It's very beautiful," I said.

My wife sighed. "I know."

"There's a lot of pressure, without the camera."

"We have to remember it all."

"But there's so much."

"I see it, and I feel like it's passing out of my head. It's there for a second, and then it's forgotten."

"I wish we'd brought them," I said. "Not just for the pictures. I keep having this weird thought. I keep wondering if my dad died."

"What?"

"He's fine. I have no reason to think he's dead. It's just—under normal circumstances, if he died, I would know. Immediately. I'd get a text or a call. But now I can't know. He could be dead right now, and I'd have to wait until we get back to the hotel to find out."

"He's probably not dead."

"I know. Still. I wish we'd brought the phones."

"But then—"

"I know."

"We'll bring them tomorrow."

"To the tower."

"To the tower."

The water fell on our feet, and the rainbows continued to burst.

●●●

When we came back to the room that night, the first thing we did was go to the safe.

"Can I tell you something?" said my wife. "This is *my* weird thought. On the boat, I started thinking about our phones. I started to worry that they had been stolen."

Her words made me feel something strange—a vibration at the top of my spine. "That would be terrible," I said.

"Of course. But I kept thinking about it. I imagined the maid getting into the safe, taking them."

"And?"

"That's it. They'd be gone. We wouldn't know what happened to them."

"That's awful. Our pictures, our happy memories—gone."

We stood there, looking at the safe. I entered the combination, the door swung open, and there they were—our phones, safe and unstolen.

I exhaled—and realized I had been holding my breath.

● ● ●

It was our last day in Charivaria. We were going to the tower.

The tower was on the eastern coast of the island. It was surrounded by a nature preserve—miles of forest and hills. We would have to hike a few hours to reach the tower. But that only made it better, rarer, more perfect. We would work for it, we would quest like knights, and we would feel it, fully. We would storm the tower and win our beloved—who was, after all, ourselves.

We laced up our hiking boots. We packed sandwiches. We charged our phones.

● ● ●

We took a bus across the island. The entrance to the preserve was a big wooden arch, and behind it were miles of green.

A notice board showed all the different paths. They crossed and recrossed each other. Some went down toward the sea, others toward the caves to the north, but one struck out eastward and upward.

We knew which path was ours. We passed under the arch and into the forest.

At first, we walked side-by-side, but the path narrowed as it rose. My wife went first, and I followed. The ground got steeper and steeper, and soon we were walking almost bent-over.

After an hour or so, we stopped to rest. We sat on a flat rock and sucked water from our bottles. The forest was quiet, but I heard the sound of my own blood, pumping through my head.

We hiked for a few more hours. When we got hungry, we sat in the hollow of a big tree and ate our sandwiches. We didn't speak much: there wasn't much we needed to say. I could still hear the beat of my blood, and that was enough.

We climbed, and soon we smelled the salt of the sea.

●●●

The path came to a stream and divided. One fork followed the stream, sloping gently down. The other fork kept climbing. And so did we. We climbed. The path was almost vertical, and we pulled ourselves up by roots and branches. We scratched and blistered our hands, and the sweat ran down into our eyes.

Suddenly, it was there.

The tower surprised us. A part of me, I think, never expected to reach it. But there it was, huge and white, pushing itself up into the sky, the sea all spread behind it.

We stood there, staring, breathing hard.

We were alone. We had only seen a few other hikers, crossing our path as they went down to the sea. We were the only ones climbing. We were here, and the tower was ours.

The door was small—its handle was an iron ring. We pulled it together, stooped, and entered the tower.

Above us, spiraling upward forever, were stairs. They ran along the sides of the tower, as far as we could see.

I smiled at my wife, and she smiled at me. We raced to the top.

●●●

It was a tie. Together, we came out of the staircase and into the open air.

The top of the tower had no roof. A low stone wall—a

parapet? wasn't this called a parapet?—was the only thing between us and the big world below. The sun was huge and hot: it seemed to be just a few feet away.

We braced ourselves against the parapet and panted. We tried to catch our breaths, but then we looked. We *saw*.

Beneath us were hundreds of feet of smooth stone tower, and beneath that hundreds of feet of cliff face, and beneath that, finally, the sea. Miles and miles of it, in all directions. Charivaria was a speck. The world was there, Spain to Jerusalem. The horizon seemed to bend, as if we were seeing the curve of the earth. We had seen things from above, of course. We had been in airplanes. But we had never seen them like this—out in the air, a little point suspended above everything.

We couldn't catch our breath after that.

I felt every drop of blood of my body, flowing perfectly through every vein and every artery.

"We're here," I said.

"We're really here."

We knew what we had to do.

We used my phone. I held it in my left hand and raised my arm as high as I could. I centered our faces and then tilted the phone up and down, trying to catch the whole horizon. The wind tugged at the phone, but I held tight.

We looked at the picture immediately. We bent over the phone and stared. My body was covered in sweat, and it seemed to freeze all at once. I shivered.

There they were, with their beautiful faces, their perfect teeth, their smiles, their huge blue world. There they were, still—that happy couple.

I could already see the likes and comments rolling in.

"I want to be there," I said.

"We *are* there," said my wife. "What did we do wrong?"

"I thought I was feeling it. My heart was racing. I could feel all my blood."

"I had goosebumps. My teeth were tingling."

"But it wasn't like *this*. It wasn't like the picture."

"Maybe if we zoom in," said my wife. She pinched the screen, and the faces got bigger. She pinched and pinched, and soon the picture showed just a few pixels of someone's tooth.

She kept pinching.

"That's not helping," I said.

"It makes me feel better."

"Well, do it on your own phone."

"Why?"

"It's—I don't know. It's annoying. I'm annoyed. I'm trying to think of how to solve this, and you're being distracting."

"You're trying to solve it? What's your solution?"

"I don't know. I haven't thought of anything yet. But if you'd stop zooming in for one second—"

She looked me in the eye, and pinched the picture.

I felt sick. We were fighting—on our honeymoon, in our tower. We had already had the happiest day of our lives, and we hadn't even felt it. This would be the rest of our lives—looking at these pictures, pinching our phones, clicking through slideshows, forgetting unforgettable places.

And then, the miracle.

She pinched again, and I pulled the phone away from her—hard. Too hard. One second it was in my sweaty fingers, and then it wasn't.

My heart jumped.

We leaned over the parapet and watched it glide downward. Ten, fifteen, twenty seconds it fell, until it bounced off the cliff, splashed into the sea, and was gone.

My pictures, my apps, my life, my self.

My chest felt hollow—as if my lungs and stomach had

gone into the sea as well. Cool air swirled through my empty insides. It didn't feel good, but it didn't feel bad either.

We stared down into the sea for a long time and then looked at each other. The woman who had been pinching the phone was gone. So too was my wife. There was someone else there.

"Oh, no," she said. "How terrible."

"Awful."

"All those pictures, gone." She was smiling.

"But we still have your phone." My cheeks were burning—I was smiling too.

"Oh, good." She took it out of her pocket. "Let's take another one."

"We have to be careful."

"Of course. Very careful."

"Let's get another angle this time."

"I was thinking the same thing." She leaned over the parapet, holding her phone out in front of her. "Something like this?"

"Exactly. But let me help you. You don't want to drop it."

I stood behind her and put my arms over hers. Our fingers braided over the phone. We leaned forward, together, and felt the wind.

The phone was in our fingers, and then it wasn't. We watched it hit the side of the tower and break into pieces. The case went one way, the screen another, and the SIM card fluttered off in the wind.

"Whoops," she said.

"We're both clumsy."

"It's terrible."

"Awful."

She had turned to me. Our faces were very close, and I felt the heat of her cheeks and her mouth.

We were not happy, but now we understood: we had not wanted to be happy. We were grinning, hugely.

The Holy Family

Our son was born with teeth. Three of them—two canines and a molar.

My wife and I were worried. The doctor reassured us. Natal teeth, she said, were perfectly normal. They were rare—only one in five thousand babies had them—but harmless.

"He's just a little ahead of the curve," said the doctor.

It was strange, at first. I nearly dropped him in the delivery room: I was shocked to see such big teeth in such tiny gums. For the first few days, my stomach sank every time he opened his mouth.

But he was our son. He had come from us. He was the product of our love, and we loved him. So we loved his teeth.

Soon, it was the other babies in the playgroup who made my stomach sink. Their pink gums seemed too smooth, and their toothless mouths seemed empty. They gummed at their pacifiers; our son grinned and laughed and bit and chewed. My wife and I were very happy. Our son was one in five thousand.

We changed our Facebook profile pictures to pictures of him. Mine was a close-up of his huge three-toothed smile; my wife's showed him in his bath, splashing me with water, laughing. I had never understood why parents did this, but now I did.

All parents think that their child is special. But we were lucky: we *knew* it.

•••

One Friday night, we had another couple over for dinner—my wife's college roommate and her husband. We were all very good friends.

They had a little boy too. Atticus was a few months older than our son, although the two were about the same size. There was nothing wrong with that, of course: our son was big and healthy, and Atticus was small for his age. But he was a perfectly fine boy, and his parents loved him very much.

I put the playpen in the dining room, and we sat at the table, ate our pasta, and watched the boys play. They were learning to stand. They grabbed the walls of the playpen, pulled themselves up, stood there, shaking, and fell backwards onto their bottoms.

We agreed: they were amazing.

After dinner, my wife's college roommate told an anecdote about breastfeeding. Atticus, she said, always fell asleep as he was nursing. We all laughed. "Do you have this problem too?" she asked my wife.

"We decided to bottle-feed him," said my wife.

"Because of, you know, all the teeth," I said.

My wife's college roommate nodded and stuck out her bottom lip. She was very sympathetic. She was sorry, she said, for my wife and my son. Breastfeeding was such a wonderful connection between a mother and her child.

"We get it in other ways," said my wife. "We have a very good connection."

Her college roommate nodded a few times. We all looked

at the boys pulling themselves up on the walls of the playpen.

"Do you give him any formula?" I said.

"Sometimes," said her college roommate's husband. "Rarely."

"Ah," said my wife.

"Why?" said her college roommate.

"I've heard doctors recommend it even to women who breastfeed," said my wife. "If their milk doesn't have enough— you know—nutrition. It might explain why Atticus is small for his age."

"He's within the normal range," said my wife's college roommate. "For height *and* weight."

My wife said she was glad to hear it: she had been worried about the little guy. We all watched the boys again. Atticus pulled himself up and held the playpen tight.

My wife's college roommate's husband announced that they were planning a trip to Paris. It would be Atticus's first time abroad.

"Aren't you worried," I said, "about taking a baby on that long of a flight?"

"Oh no," said my wife's college roommate. Her eyes got very big. "Atticus is a good boy. He hardly ever cries."

"Even if he did," said her husband, "we'd still take him. It's important for kids to have experiences like that. Good for their development, to be exposed to different cultures."

"Their brains are like sponges at this age," said my wife's college roommate. "They soak up everything."

"Of course," I said. We watched the boys again. I raised an eyebrow at my wife, and she frowned. We had never considered going abroad. We had failed our son.

Almost.

"It's interesting," said my wife, "that you chose Paris."

"Why?" said her college roommate. "Paris is wonderful."

"Oh no, of course. It's perfectly nice. It's just—you know."

My wife's college roommate's eyes got big again. "No," she said. "I don't know."

"It's wonderful, of course. But for our trip, we were hoping for something more creative."

"Creative?"

"The whole 'Americans going to Paris for *culture*' thing— it's been done. We're going to take our son abroad too, obviously, but we've been waiting for the right place. We want it to be really special."

I had never loved my wife more than I did at that moment. I was ashamed that I had only given her one beautiful son.

"Well, of course," said her college roommate. "We've been to plenty of special places." She and her husband started to tell us about them—a semester in Naples, a summer building low-emission wood-burning stoves in Costa Rica. They were interrupted by crying. The boys had tried to pull themselves up on the same part of the playpen, but it was only wide enough for one little hand. They slapped at each other and swayed, and our son held the fence. Atticus fell backward, hit the carpet, opened his little toothless mouth, and wailed.

● ● ●

That night, my wife and I stayed up late. We lay next to each other in bed, looking at our phones, searching for our special place.

We read lists—"Top 10 Undiscovered Gems!" "12 Places You Won't Even Believe Exist!" "17 Most Unique Destinations to See Before You Die!" We clicked through slideshows, and saw pictures of Iceland and Laos and Patagonia.

None of them were right. My boss had gone to Iceland a

few years ago. My wife's cousin had worked for a development NGO in Laos. One of my uncles had taken a Patagonian cruise. No—we needed something special.

We found Werdenburg.

It was number eight on "Not Your Parents' Europe! Nine Amazing Places Off the Beaten Path." My wife and I had never heard of it. We started to get excited.

Werdenburg, said the article, was once a jewel of central Europe. Located east of Vienna and west of Prague, it had once been the third great city of the Habsburg empire. Mozart debuted some of his early symphonies in Werdenburg, and Rilke wrote a series of poems called the *Werdenburg Sonnets*. The world wars and communism left the city in ruins, but since the nineties, it had been rebuilding. Werdenburg Castle had been restored, the Springbrunnen palace had reopened to tourists, and the city's looted art was returned and placed in a new ultramodern museum. The cathedral bell once again rang in the morning, and baroque masterpieces hung in Werdenburg for the first time in decades.

Atticus and his parents could stand with the other Americans in front of the *Mona Lisa*. We had Werdenburg.

● ● ●

We went at the end of June. Our son was walking now, with hardly any help. His molar and two canines had been joined by a full set of teeth, and he showed them off whenever he could. He was a very happy boy, and he had very happy parents.

As we waited for the plane to take off, we took some pictures. I got a good one of my son wearing the in-flight headphones and grinning. I posted it on Facebook—"His first international flight!" I wrote. Dozens of my friends liked it—

how could you not?—but my wife and I couldn't help noticing that Atticus's parents didn't. It was too bad: we had liked all of their Eiffel Tower selfies.

The flight attendant asked us if we needed anything for the baby. She said we were brave to take such a little one on such a long flight. My wife and I shook our heads. We weren't brave—we were just doing our duty.

We walked up and down the taxi line at the Werdenburg airport: none of the drivers had a car seat. "It's okay," said one. "I'm very careful."

We piled into his backseat, and I held my son against my chest. After a while, my wife told me to loosen my grip: his face was getting a little purple.

The taxi got onto the highway and drove toward Werdenburg. We passed miles of apartment buildings—long white blocks of communist concrete. Soon we were in the city itself, bouncing over the cobblestones and dodging the trams. We had driven, it seemed, into the eighteenth century: the buildings were painted light blue and lemon and rose-pink, and complicated crests hung over the windows and the tall wooden doors. My wife told me to hold our son up to the window so he could see. That was, after all, why were here.

I pulled him closer to my chest and leaned toward the window. We looked out at the city, and he pounded the window with his little fist. I smiled at my wife. He was so strong, and he was ready.

That afternoon, we went to the Springbrunnen Palace.

TripAdvisor said it was one of the highlights of Werdenburg—a pristine example of late baroque architecture, even more sumptuous than Versailles.

We walked up and down the long gilded galleries, beneath a ceiling painted to look like the sky. We looked into the bedroom of Maximilian VI, and we took a picture in front of the bronze statue of Apollo.

In each room were laminated cards that described the objects and architecture. We picked them up and learned about the cornices and chairs. My son was in his carrier, strapped to my chest, facing outward so he could see the palace. We read the cards to him.

"Look," I said. We were in the Hall of Mirrors, leaning over the empress's own harpsichord. A double-headed eagle was painted in gold on the lid. "Do you see that? That's the symbol of the Austro-Hungarian empire."

He wriggled in his carrier.

"Their brains are like sponges at this age," said my wife.

After lunch, we went outside, into the gardens. They had been restored to their original glory—the neat, elaborate hedges, the sundial made of flowers, the white peacocks, the bronze statues of nymphs and fauns. My wife and I agreed: it was definitely more sumptuous than Versailles.

Our son got antsy and kicked me in the stomach a couple times, so we let him out of his carrier. He tottered through the gardens, chasing the peacocks. We took pictures and videos.

I had never been happier. I was always happy, of course: I loved him, and I knew how special he was. But it made me especially happy to be with him *here*, in a place that was as special as he was.

That night, back at the hotel, my wife and I watched our videos and compared our pictures. She had taken a good one: he had caught a peacock and was tugging at its tail-feathers. I made it my profile picture.

•••

The next morning we went to the Kunstmuseum. I was wearing the carrier on my chest again. I paid for an audio guide, and as we walked through the museum, I listened to facts about the paintings and repeated them to my son.

"Look," I said. We were in front of a little square painting, framed in gold. "This is an altarpiece from the old Werdenburg Cathedral. That's the crucifixion there, in the center panel. And there's the Virgin and Mary Magdalene and St. John."

I pointed my chest up, toward at the painting, so he could see their little pained faces.

The museum had eight centuries of Werdenburger art. We moved through the rooms, and the flat medieval saints changed into muscular Renaissance men. Soon we were in the seventeenth century—the late baroque masterpieces that the internet had promised us. My wife stopped in front of a little picture of the annunciation. My son and I went to the big canvas on the opposite wall.

It was called *The Holy Family*. At the center of the picture was the child—a big baby with gold curls and red cheeks. He gazed at heaven and smiled wisely. On either side were his parents. Mary supported the child from behind and offered him her breast—Joseph was on his knees, hands clutching his chest, before his son. Above their heads, heaven burst with doves and cherubs.

The Holy Family, said the audio guide, was the treasure of the Kunstmuseum's collection. Painted by Matteo Settembrini, an Italian in the service of the Duke of Werdenburg, it had been looted by the Red Army in 1945. After twenty years of negotiations, the painting had been returned from Moscow last year. It was the finest surviving instance of Settembrini's religious work: his sensitive brushstrokes brought real emotion to a conventional scene.

I repeated all this to my son. It was so true: I didn't know what made a brushstroke sensitive, but I knew those emotions—the pride, the joy, the wonder, the love. I felt them in every curl of the child's hair, in every dove's feather.

I took two steps toward the painting. I could see the grain of the canvas, the cracks of the paint. I put my face very close and stared deep into those sensitive brushstrokes.

I felt my son squirm in his carrier, and heard a little plunk.

Joseph was gone. His face had become a hole. My son waved his fist.

● ● ●

Two museum guards led us through a door marked ZUTRITT VERBOTEN—DO NOT ENTER. We walked down a long white hallway hung with abstract paintings. At the end was a big office that overlooked the museum courtyard. The guards told us to wait here—the director would see us soon. We sat in some very geometric chairs, and the guards shut the door behind them.

My wife held our son on her lap. She started to speak, but I stopped her. "Their brains are like sponges at this age," I said. She put her hands over his ears, and we whispered:

"You're sure it was him?"

"Who else would it be?"

"Maybe it was like that when we got here."

"You heard it."

"It's not like him. He's a good boy."

"It's my fault. He didn't know. He's just a baby."

I said it, but I knew it wasn't true. He wasn't just a baby. He was special—he was *ours*.

"Atticus didn't punch any Cézannes in Paris," said my wife.

"That we know of, anyway."

I stared out into the courtyard. It had started to drizzle, and the abstract sculptures were wet and shiny.

"Maybe it won't be a big deal."

"No one has even heard of Werdenburg."

"The damage wasn't that bad."

"It wasn't like he hit the Christ child. It's just Joseph."

"What happens in Werdenburg stays in Werdenburg."

We both looked at our son. He put his fist into his mouth. I noticed a little blotch of brown on his wrist—a bit of Joseph's beard.

●●●

The director was a small woman with short gray hair. She asked us a few questions, and we answered. My wife kept her hands over our son's ears.

The director told us that the painting was insured, and that the curators hoped it could be restored. "However," she said, "this particular painting is quite important to the city. It took twenty years of negotiations, and several millions of dollars, to get it back from Russia. And so there must be some consequences."

My wife pulled our son to her chest. My stomach sank.

"It was an accident," I said.

"You really shouldn't let people get so close to the art," said my wife.

"We are asking," said the director, "for you to pay some of the cost of the restoration." She told us how much. It was a lot. The museum would announce that we were paying for the painting, but it would not release our names to public. "We think that this is an appropriate compromise between consequences for your actions and, well, your safety."

"Safety?"

"Some people in Werdenburg will be angry. And there is, of course, the internet." She told us that people who had damaged art at other museums had been harassed and threatened by trolls.

My wife and I nodded several times. We were very serious. But the muscles at the corners of our mouths burned: we were trying not to smile.

We were happy to pay for the restoration: we already had more debt than we could ever pay—student loans, credit cards, a mortgage—so what difference did a painting make? We would go back to America, send the Kunstmuseum a few dollars a month, and leave the whole thing in Werdenburg.

Everything was fine: *The Holy Family* would be restored.

●●●

I locked the hotel-room door behind us and drew the chain. My wife put our son on the bed and turned on the TV. She nodded, and I followed her into the bathroom, away from the sponge-brain.

"What do we do?" I said. "Is it safe for us to stay here?"

"What else can we do?"

"Go home?"

"And what do we say when people ask us why we left Werdenburg early?"

I filled a glass of water from the sink and looked at it. "We'll tell them he got sick."

"He never gets sick."

That was true: he was a very healthy baby. "We'll say the

food didn't agree with him."

"Plenty of babies travel. Of course he can travel."

I sat on the edge of the tub. "Well, what else can we do? We can't just stay here."

She looked at me.

"Can we?" I said.

"Why not? The museum didn't release our names. We're not in any danger."

"So we stay a few more days and leave at the normal time."

"And everything's normal."

I really did love this woman.

● ● ●

That afternoon, we went to the Werdenburg Cathedral. It was on the east side of St. Joseph's Square, across from our hotel. We walked up and down the nave, and into all the little chapels, lined with elaborate marble tombs carved with scrolls and skulls. We climbed to the top of the bell-tower and looked down at the bright orange tiles of the city's roofs. My wife wore the carrier, and I watched our son's arms. Everything was normal.

We left the cathedral and walked back to our hotel. When we were halfway across the square, we saw a big crowd outside the hotel. Men were standing around, smoking. Some of them had big professional cameras around their necks.

Before we understood, they were on us—surrounding us, taking pictures, shouting about *das baby*. My wife covered our son's face with her arms. "Hey!" I shouted at the photographers. "Hey! Stop!"

We took a few steps backwards, and so did they. I turned and ran, and my wife followed. The cathedral rose in front of us.

We sat in one of the chapels, panting. The setting sun came in bright through the stained glass window—our faces were red and yellow and blue.

We were safe, for now: the photographers hadn't followed us into the church. We looked at the internet on our phones.

Someone had leaked the museum's security footage. I watched it a few times: I stood there, squinting at *The Holy Family*, while my son smiled and punched a hole through the canvas.

BuzzFeed, Huffington Post, NPR, CNN, BBC, *The New York Times*, *The Guardian*—everyone had a story about it. Reddit had figured out our names and posted our Facebook profiles. #HoleyFamily was the number one topic on Twitter.

And then there were the memes. People had taken a freeze-frame of the video—our son, at the moment his fist hit the canvas, smiling, showing all his beautiful teeth—and photoshopped it into other pictures. I scrolled through Twitter, and saw my son punch at everything—other famous paintings, Mike Tyson, the Minions. Someone had even put him into 9/11. His fist was the second plane.

I had hundreds of DMs and notifications. I grabbed at my stomach: that seemed to be the only way to keep it from sinking out of my body and through the floor of the church. I shut off my phone, leaned against one of the marble tombs, and closed my eyes. My son pulled hard at my leg hair. I picked him up and held him very close.

My wife went to the door and came back. The photographers were there, waiting.

"Maybe we can claim sanctuary here," I said. "Like in that cartoon—*The Hunchback of Notre Dame*." I rubbed my cheek against the cold marble. "Maybe we never have to leave."

"No one in this family is a hunchback." She looked up at the stained glass window. "We shouldn't have to hide. What did we do to deserve this? Love our son? Try to give him a good experience? To help his development?"

"He did punch the painting."

"So? Do we love him less?"

I looked down at him. He had my eyes, and her nose—and all those teeth. No—I would never not love him.

Suddenly, I understood. My heart started to beat very fast, and the back of my neck tingled. We had forgotten the most obvious, most important thing.

"Maybe," I said, "it was a good thing."

"What?"

"Think about it. The city wanted to be better known, to have more tourists. Now everyone in the world knows about Werdenburg."

"People are going to come from all over to see that painting now."

"All because he punched it."

"They should be thanking us, really."

"It's just like the teeth."

"We were frightened at first. But then it was alright—it was better, even."

"No one else has ever had a trip like this.

"No, no—Atticus didn't punch a Cézanne."

"Of course he didn't. He isn't that special."

"There's no other boy in the world who has a mob waiting to take his picture!"

She rushed over to me, and we embraced, our son between us. We buried our faces in his cheeks.

• • •

The photographers were still there, outside the big wooden door of the cathedral. As soon as I touched the handle, the cameras began to click.

We walked toward them, slowly, together—me and my wife, holding our son between us. A part of me wanted to run back into the cathedral—the same panic flashed across my wife's pale face. We looked down at our son. He was waving his fists at the camera flashes, grinning and happy. He was our son, and we loved him. The cameras kept clicking, and we showed the world our big smiles, full of teeth.

About the Author

RYAN NAPIER's stories have appeared in *Entropy*, *Noble / Gas Qtrly*, *Queen Mob's Tea House*, *minor literature[s]*, and others. He lives in Massachusetts.

More information at ryannapier.net.

This book was published with assistance from the Spring 2018 Editing and Publishing class at the University of North Carolina at Chapel Hill. Contributing editors and designers were Ann Bingham, Isabella Bonner, Neecole Bostick, Bryant Chappell, Griffin Deadwick, Sofie DeWulf, Christian Gibson, Emily Jarrett, Robby Pierce, Callie Riek, Quincy Rife, Madison Schaper, Emma Sims, Matthew Skipper, Grace Towery, and Molly Weybright.